CALICO ILLUSTRATED CLASSICS

Charles Dickens's

A Tale of Two Cities

ADAPTED BY: Karen Kelly
ILLUSTRATED BY: Ute Simon

magic
wagon

visit us at www.abdopublishing.com

Published by Magic Wagon, a division of the ABDO Group,
8000 West 78th Street, Edina, Minnesota 55439. Copyright
© 2010 by Abdo Consulting Group, Inc. International copyrights
reserved in all countries. All rights reserved. No part of this
book may be reproduced in any form without written permission
from the publisher.

Calico Chapter Books™ is a trademark and logo of Magic Wagon.

Printed in the United States of America, Melrose Park, Illinois.
102009
012010

 PRINTED ON RECYCLED PAPER

Original text by Charles Dickens
Adapted by Karen Kelly
Illustrated by Ute Simon
Edited by Stephanie Hedlund and Rochelle Baltzer
Cover and interior design by Jaime Martens

Library of Congress Cataloging-in-Publication Data

Kelly, Karen, 1962-
   A tale of two cities / adapted by Karen Kelly ; illustrated by Ute
Simon ; based on the works of Charles Dickens.
      p. cm. -- (Calico illustrated classics)
   ISBN 978-1-60270-712-2
   1. France--History--Revolution, 1789-1799--Juvenile fiction. [1.
France--History--Revolution, 1789-1799--Fiction. 2. Friendship--
Fiction. 3. Loyalty--Fiction. 4. Revenge--Fiction.] I. Simon, Ute, ill. II.
Dickens, Charles, 1812-1870. Tale of two cities. III. Title.
   PZ7.K29632Tal 2010
   [Fic]--dc22
                                                       2009033966

Table of Contents

The Period

It was the best of times. It was the worst of times. It was the season of light. It was the season of darkness. It was the spring of hope. It was the winter of despair.

The horses mashed their way through thick mud with drooping heads. They were pulling the Dover mail coach up Shooter's Hill. It was late on a Friday night in November 1775. The hill, the harness, the mud, and the mail were all so heavy that the horses had already stopped three times.

A cold mist had roamed up the hill like an evil spirit. Three passengers were plodding up the hill by the side of the mail. They could only see a few yards of road from the light of the coach lamps. In those days, travelers kept to themselves, for anyone on the road might be a robber.

The guard of the Dover mail stood watch with a loaded blunderbuss, six or eight loaded pistols, and a pile of swords at hand.

"Joe!" said the coachman. "What o'clock do you make it, Joe?"

"Ten minutes past eleven."

"My blood!" exclaimed the coachman. "And not atop of Shooter's yet! Get on with you!" He added the whip to emphasize his command.

The lead horse made a determined scramble and the three other horses followed. This last burst carried the mail to the summit of the hill. When the horses stopped to breathe again, the guard got down off the coach. He opened the coach door to let the passengers back in.

"Tst! Joe!" cried the coachman in a warning voice from his perch on the box. Both men listened. The sound of a galloping horse came fast and furious up the hill.

"So-ho!" the guard sang out, as loud as he could roar. "You there! Stand! I shall fire!"

The gallop quickly slowed and a man's voice called from the mist. "Is that the Dover mail?"

"Never you mind!" the guard retorted. "Why do you want to know?"

"I want a passenger, if it is."

"What passenger?"

"Mr. Jarvis Lorry."

One passenger showed in a moment that was his name. The guard, the coachman, and the two other passengers looked at him full of distrust.

"Keep where you are," the guard called to the voice in the mist. "Gentleman named Lorry answer straight."

"What is the matter?" asked the passenger. "Is it Jerry?"

"Yes, Mr. Lorry. A bulletin sent you from over yonder. T. and Company."

"I know this messenger, guard," said Mr. Lorry. He climbed down onto the road. "He may come close. There's nothing wrong."

"I hope there ain't," said the guard. "Hello you! Come close slowly."

A horse and rider came carefully through the mist to the passenger. The rider stooped and handed him a small folded paper.

Lorry opened the paper in the light of the coach lamp and read aloud, "'Wait at Dover for Mam'selle.' Jerry, say my answer was, recalled to life."

Jerry started in his saddle. "That's a blazing strange answer."

"Take that message back and they will understand." The passenger opened the coach door and got in.

The coach lumbered on again with wreaths of mist closing around it as it began to head downhill. Jerry dismounted his spent horse and turned to walk it down the other side of the hill.

He muttered to himself, "Recalled to life. Blazing strange message! You'd be in a blazing bad way, if recalling to life was to come into fashion, Jerry!"

Night Shadows

The mail coach lumbered, jolted, rattled, and bumped its way toward Dover. In the shadows, the three passengers gave in to dozing. The passenger from the bank dreamed all night that he was on his way to dig someone out of a grave.

A hundred times the dozing passenger asked the spirit, "Buried how long?" The answer was always the same. "Almost eighteen years."

"You know you are recalled to life?"

"They tell me so."

After these words were spoken, the passenger would dig and dig. When the wretched man was out of the grave at last, he would suddenly fall away to dust.

The weary passenger finally awoke and found the shadows of the night were gone.

When the mail coach got successfully to Dover, the head waiter at the Royal George Hotel opened the door with a flourish. Mr. Lorry came out of the coach, shaking straw from his coat rather like a large dog.

Awhile later, Mr. Lorry sat alone in the coffee room dressed in a formal brown suit. He wore an odd little flaxen wig.

When the waiter brought breakfast, Mr. Lorry said, "I wish rooms prepared for a young lady who may come here today. She may ask for Mr. Jarvis Lorry or for a gentleman from Tellson's Bank. Please to let me know."

"Yes, sir. Tellson's Bank in London, sir?"

"Yes," Mr. Lorry confirmed.

The day had declined into dark when the waiter came to announce Miss Manette had arrived from London. He said she would be happy to see Mr. Lorry. The gentleman adjusted his little wig and followed the waiter.

Mr. Lorry saw a young lady of not more than seventeen standing by a table. His eyes rested on her blond hair, blue eyes, and slight, pretty figure. He made a formal bow to Miss Manette.

"Pray take a seat, sir." Miss Manette had a clear, pleasant voice with a little foreign accent.

Mr. Lorry bowed again and took his seat.

"I received a letter from the bank yesterday, informing me there was some discovery about my poor father so long dead. The bank told me you would explain the details to me and to prepare myself for their surprising nature. I am naturally eager to know what they are."

"It is very difficult to begin." He paused. "Miss Manette, I am a man of business. I will relate to you a story of one of our customers."

"A story!"

"Yes. He was a French gentleman. A scientific man of great accomplishment and a doctor, like your father. I speak of twenty years ago, miss. He married an English lady and I took care of his business affairs.

"He silently disappeared. He had an enemy in some countryman, who had the power to send someone to prison for any length of time.

His wife begged the king, the queen, and the court for any tidings of him in vain."

"This doctor's wife was a lady of great courage. But she had suffered so intensely from this that she determined to spare her child—"

"A girl?"

"Yes, a girl. Therefore, she raised her daughter in the belief that her father was dead. Miss Manette, your mother took this course with you. You had no dark cloud of worry about whether your father died in prison—"

The expression on Miss Manette's face had deepened into one of pain and horror.

"He has been found alive. Greatly changed, it is most likely. Your father has been taken to the house of an old servant in Paris. We are going there. I will identify him, if I can. You will restore him to life, love, rest, and comfort."

A shiver ran through Miss Manette's frame. She said in a low voice, "It will be his ghost, not him!"

Mr. Lorry rubbed her hands. "There, there! The best and worst are known to you now.

With a fair sea voyage and a fair land journey, you will be soon at his side. What is the matter? Miss Manette!"

Her eyes were open and fixed upon him and yet not seeing. So tight was her grip on his arm that he feared it would hurt her to move. He called out loudly for assistance.

A wild-looking woman with red hair and a most wonderful bonnet ran into the room. She laid a brawny hand on Mr. Lorry's chest and sent him flying back against the nearest wall.

The woman yelled out to the inn servants nearby, "Why don't you go fetch things, instead of standing there staring? Bring smelling-salts, cold water, and vinegar, quick!"

She softly settled the patient on the sofa, tending her with great skill and gentleness.

"And you in brown!" she said, turning to Mr. Lorry. "Couldn't you tell her what you had to tell her without frightening her to death?"

Mr. Lorry was so bewildered by her question he could only look from a distance as the strong woman nursed her young mistress. Soon Miss Manette was strong enough to sit up a little.

"I hope she will do well now," he said.

"No thanks to you, if she does!"

"I hope that you accompany Miss Manette to France?" Mr. Lorry said feebly.

"A likely thing, too!" replied the woman.

The Wine Shop

In the Paris suburb of Saint Antoine a large cask of red wine tumbled out of a cart. It lay on the narrow stone street in front of the wine shop like a shattered walnut shell.

All the people within sight stopped to run and drink the wine. The rough stones of the street had created little wine pools. Men, women, and children scooped, dipped, and sipped all they could, along with much mud.

A shrill sound of laughter and play echoed in the street. Everyone joined in the fun. When the wine was gone, the fun was also. The people went back to their hard lives as before but with their hands, feet, and faces stained red.

The wine shop was a corner shop and better than most in Saint Antoine. The owner stood outside to watch the struggle for the lost wine. His eyes caught a tall man writing on a wall. He called to him across the way. "My Gaspard, what do you do there?"

The fellow pointed to the wall where he had written *blood* with his finger dipped in muddy wine.

"Are you ready for the mad hospital?" asked the shopkeeper. He crossed the road and smeared over the word with a handful of mud. He wiped his soiled hand on the man's shirt and went back to his wine shop.

This shopkeeper was a bull-necked man of thirty years. His shirt sleeves were rolled up and showed strong, brown arms. He wore nothing more on his head than his own curling short, dark hair.

Madame Defarge, his wife, sat in the shop behind the counter as he came in. She was a stout woman with a watchful eye. A bright shawl was twined about her head but did not cover her large earrings. Her knitting lay before her.

She said nothing to her husband but coughed one tiny cough and lifted her dark brows. The shopkeeper shifted his eyes about the store until he found an older gentleman and a young lady seated in a corner.

Madame Defarge took up her knitting and became absorbed in it. The gentleman advanced from the corner and asked to speak with Monsieur Defarge.

"Willingly, sir," said Monsieur Defarge and they quietly stepped to the door.

Their talk was very short. Monsieur Defarge became very attentive. Then he nodded and went out. The gentleman motioned to the young lady and they went out also. They met Monsieur Defarge in a gloomy entry to a gloomy staircase.

"It is very high. It is a little difficult," Monsieur Defarge said to Mr. Lorry. They began climbing the stairs.

"Is he alone?" Mr. Lorry whispered.

"Who should be with him?" said the man.

"He is greatly changed?"

"Changed!" The keeper of the wine shop stopped to strike the wall with his hand.

Mr. Lorry's spirits grew heavier and heavier as they climbed. At last they reached the very top of the building to the last door. The keeper of the wine shop took out a key.

"The door is locked, then, my friend?" said Mr. Lorry, surprised.

"Yes," was the grim reply.

"You think it necessary to keep the gentleman so? Why?"

"Because he has lived so long locked up. He would be frightened, tear himself to pieces, die even, if his door was left open."

"Is it possible?" exclaimed Mr. Lorry.

"Yes," repeated Defarge, bitterly.

Monsieur Defarge struck the door two or three times for no other reason but to make noise. Then he drew the key across the door several times before putting it in the lock. The door opened slowly and he looked into the room. He beckoned them to enter. Mr. Lorry put his arm around the daughter.

"Come in, come in," Lorry urged.

"I am afraid of him, of my father," she answered, shuddering.

Feeling desperate, he lifted her a little and hurried her into the room.

Such a small amount of light was in the room that it was difficult to see. Yet a white-haired man sat on a low bench. He was stooped forward and very busy, making shoes.

"Good day!" said Monsieur Defarge, looking down at the white head.

It rose for a moment and a very faint voice responded, "Good day!"

"You are still hard at work?"

"Yes. I am working." The voice was so sunken it sounded like a voice underground.

Defarge said, "I want to let in a little more light. You can bear a little more?"

The shoemaker stopped his work. "I must bear it, if you let it in."

A broad ray of light fell into the room. The light showed the workman with an unfinished shoe on his lap. His few tools and various scraps of leather were at his feet and on his bench. He had a ragged white beard, a hollow face, and extremely bright eyes.

Mr. Lorry came silently forward.

"You have a visitor," said Monsieur Defarge.

The shoemaker looked up but continued working on the shoe.

"Tell monsieur what kind of shoe it is and the maker's name."

"It is a young lady's walking shoe." He glanced at the shoe with a touch of pride.

"And the maker's name?" said Defarge.

"One Hundred and Five, North Tower." With a weary sound, he bent silently to his work again.

Mr. Lorry said to the shoemaker, "Monsieur Manette, do you remember nothing of me?"

The shoe dropped to the ground and he sat looking from his old banker to his old servant. For a moment, an active intelligence showed through the black mist that had fallen on him. Then it was gone. He picked the shoe up again.

Miss Manette moved away from the wall to

very near the bench. She stood, making not a sound. When the shoemaker stooped to his work again, his eyes noticed her dress skirt. He raised his eyes and saw her face.

Breathing quickly he said, "You are not the jailer's daughter?"

She sighed, "No."

"Who are you?"

She sat down on the bench beside him. He put out his hand, took a golden curl and looked at it. Then he put his other hand to his neck and took off a folded rag hanging from a string. He opened it carefully on his knee.

Two long golden hairs lay inside. "It is the same. How can it be?" He turned her toward the light. "My little one laid her head on my shoulder, when I was called out that night. These were found after I was brought to the North Tower." He formed this speech intelligently, though slowly.

"Was it you?"

His daughter fell on her knees before him.

"Your agony is over, Father. We go to

England to be at peace and rest." He sank into her arms. "Good gentlemen, thank God!"

This sight was so touching, yet so terrible in the great wrong and suffering he had endured. The two men covered their faces.

The time to begin their journey came. His daughter drew her arm through her father's and he took her hand in both of his.

They began to descend the stairs. Monsieur

Defarge went first with the lamp and Mr. Lorry closed the small parade. On reaching the courtyard only one soul was to be seen. Madame Defarge leaned against a doorpost, knitting.

The prisoner got into a coach and his daughter and Mr. Lorry followed.

Defarge got up on the box and gave the command, "To the Barrier!" The coachman cracked his whip and they clattered away.

At the city gate, soldiers stood with lanterns at the guard house. They commanded, "Your papers, travelers!"

"See here, then, Monsieur the Officer," said Defarge. He got down and took the soldier aside. "These are the papers of the monsieur inside with the white head."

After a look inside the coach the soldier declared, "It is well. Forward!"

"Adieu!" called Defarge, as the coach went on without him under the great grove of stars.

Five Years Later

Outside Tellson's Bank by the Temple Bar law courts in London was an odd-job man who served the bank. Every morning Jerry Cruncher took up his station on a stool underneath the banking house window. Every morning his twelve-year-old son was with him.

One morning in 1780, they had just arrived to their post when a head from inside Tellson's was put out the door to give the word.

"Porter wanted!"

"Hooray, Father! Here's an early job!" Young Jerry wasted no time sitting himself on the stool after his father stood.

"You know the Old Bailey well, no doubt?" said the old clerk to Cruncher, meaning the criminal court building.

"Ye-es, sir," returned Cruncher.

"And you know Mr. Lorry."

"I know Mr. Lorry, sir," said Cruncher.

"Find the door where the witnesses go in and show the doorkeeper this note. He will let you into the court. The doorkeeper will pass the note to Mr. Lorry. Show Mr. Lorry where you stand. Then, remain there until he wants you."

"I suppose they'll be trying forgeries this morning?" Cruncher remarked.

"Treason. Here is the letter. Go along," said the old clerk.

The jail was a foul place. It was famous for the stockade, the whipping post, and the deadly diseases bred there. Making his way through the crowds, Cruncher found the door he sought. After some delay, the door turned on its hinges and he squeezed himself into court.

"What's coming on?" he asked the man next to him.

"The treason case. He'll die horribly," answered the man with approval.

"If he's found guilty, you mean," Cruncher added.

"Oh! They'll find him guilty."

Cruncher watched the doorkeeper, who was making his way to Mr. Lorry. He sat at a table near a wigged gentleman, the prisoner's attorney. Almost opposite of Mr. Lorry was another wigged gentleman with his hands in his pockets, staring at the ceiling.

Cruncher coughed, rubbed his chin, signed with his hand, and finally attracted the notice of Mr. Lorry. The businessman quietly nodded.

"What's he got to do with the case?" asked the man he was next to.

"Blest if I know," said Cruncher.

The judge entered and stopped their talk. Two jailers brought the prisoner in, while eager faces strained to see every inch of him. The object of all the staring was a young man of about twenty-five. He was plainly dressed in black and his long, dark hair was pulled back with a ribbon. He bowed to the judge.

"Silence in the court!" It was announced

Charles Darnay had yesterday pleaded not guilty to the charge that he was a false traitor to England's serene, exalted and excellent king. Not guilty of his having assisted Lewis the French king in his wars against England. Not guilty of his revealing to the French what forces England had prepared to send to Canada and North America.

The accused stood quiet and attentive with his hands resting on a slab of wood before him.

Mr. Attorney-General rose to inform the jury that the prisoner, though young in years, was old in the practice of treason. The prisoner had been passing back and forth between England and France on business.

However, there were two witnesses who would reveal the true reason for those travels. These witnesses had discovered documents among the prisoner's possessions, lists of His Majesty's forces and preparation for battles on both land and sea. For these reasons, the jury must find the prisoner guilty, whether they liked it or not.

When the Attorney-General finally stopped talking, a buzz of chatter arose in the court. When the noise died down, the first witness appeared in the witness-box. Mr. Solicitor-General examined the man.

The story of witness John Barsad was what the Attorney-General had told it to be. In fact, it was exactly the same. Mr. Barsad was ready to withdraw himself, when the gentleman sitting near Mr. Lorry begged to ask him a few questions.

Had he ever been a spy himself? No, he was insulted by the suggestion. Ever been in prison? Certainly not. Never in a debtor's prison? He didn't see what that had to do with it. How many times? Two or three. Not five or six? Perhaps. Sure he saw the prisoner with the lists? Certain. Had he in fact provided them himself? No.

The next witness, Roger Cly, gave his testimony as quickly as he could. He had begun serving the prisoner four years ago after meeting him on a Calais boat. He became suspicious of the prisoner and started watching him closely. He saw him talking to French gentlemen and showing them similar lists.

Cly had taken the lists he found in the prisoner's desk. No, he had not placed them there first. He turned in the information because he loved his country. He had known the first witness seven or eight years, but that was just a coincidence. No, he had never been suspected of stealing a silver teapot. He had been falsely accused about a mustard pot.

Mr. Attorney-General called Mr. Jarvis Lorry to testify. He seemed to want to prove the prisoner had been on the Dover mail that same misty night in 1775, but Mr. Lorry could not help him do so. Mr. Attorney-General released Mr. Lorry and called, "Miss Manette!"

The crowd buzzed again as Miss Manette stood up.

"Miss Manette, look at the prisoner." The look of pity and compassion from the young lady was clearly painful for the prisoner to see.

"Have you seen the prisoner before?"

"Yes, sir. On a ship passage across the channel."

"Tell us about it."

"When the gentleman came aboard . . ."

"Do you mean the prisoner?" asked the judge.

"Yes, my Lord."

"Then say 'the prisoner'."

"When the prisoner came aboard he noticed my father was in a weak state of health. I had made a bed for him on the deck. The prisoner was so good as to offer to show me how I could shelter my father from the wind and weather better than I had done."

The Attorney-General continued to ask questions in a way to show the prisoner's guilt. Miss Manette's answers revealed the prisoner's kindness, intelligence, and honesty.

Mr. Attorney-General then turned his questions to Doctor Manette.

"Doctor Manette, have you ever seen the prisoner before?"

"Once. When he called at my lodgings in London. Some three or so years ago."

"Can you speak about his talk with your daughter on the ship?"

"Sir, I cannot."

"Had it been your misfortune to suffer a long imprisonment without trial in your native country?"

Doctor Manette answered in a tone that went to every heart, "A very long imprisonment. My mind is a blank until a gracious God restored me and I found myself living with my dear daughter."

Another witness testified that the prisoner had been at a particular room in a particular hotel on that Friday night in November 1775. The prisoner's attorney, Mr. Stryver, was cross-examining the man with no result.

The wigged gentleman, who had all this time been looking at the ceiling, wrote on a piece of paper, twisted it up, and tossed it to Mr. Stryver. After reading the paper, he looked curiously at the prisoner.

"You say again you are quite sure it was the prisoner?"

The witness was quite sure.

"Did you ever see anyone very like the prisoner?"

The witness said, "Not so like that I could be mistaken."

"Look well upon that gentleman over there," the counsel said, pointing to the man who had tossed the paper to him. "Then look well upon the prisoner. Are they very like each other?"

Though the man was careless and grubby, the likeness between them was remarkable. This was made even more obvious when that man removed his wig. The testimony of the witness was smashed like a crockery vessel.

Mr. Stryver called his few witnesses and closing speeches were made. Then it was the jury's time to decide their verdict.

An hour and a half limped slowly by. Jerry Cruncher had dropped into a doze outside the courtroom. A loud tide of people heading back to the courtroom woke him and carried him along.

"Jerry!" Mr. Lorry was calling him when he got there. Mr. Lorry handed him a piece of paper. "Quick!"

Written on the paper was, "Not guilty."

The Jackal

Doctor Manette, Lucie Manette, Mr. Lorry, and Mr. Stryver gathered around Charles Darnay. They congratulated him on his escape from death.

"I have done my best for you, Mr. Darnay. My best is as good as another man's, I believe." Mr. Stryver was a stout, loud, red-faced man who looked twenty years older than his age.

"Much better," said Mr. Lorry, being polite. "Now, I request that we all head to our homes. Miss Lucie looks ill. Mr. Darnay has had a terrible day, and we are all worn out."

A hackney coach was called for and Doctor Manette and his daughter departed in it. Mr. Stryver left them to fight his way back to the robing room.

"Mr. Darnay, good night. I hope you have been this day preserved for a successful and happy life." Mr. Lorry waved at a chair for hire, bustled into it, and was carried off to Tellson's.

Mr. Sydney Carton, who had been leaning against the wall in the shadows, stepped up to speak to Darnay. "This is a strange chance that throws you and me together. It must be a strange night for you."

"I hardly seem to belong to this world again," returned Charles Darnay.

"You speak faintly. Let me show you the nearest tavern to dine."

Soon they were seated in a little room. Charles Darnay was gaining strength with a good plain dinner. Carton sat opposite him. When Darnay's dinner was done, Carton filled his large glass and said, "Mr. Darnay, why don't you give your toast?"

"Miss Manette, then!" Darnay held up his glass of good wine.

"Miss Manette!" Carton drank the toast and then flung his glass over his shoulder against the wall. He ordered another glass and filled his new goblet.

"Mr. Darnay, let me ask you a question before you go. Do you think I like you?"

"You have acted as if you do. But I don't think you do."

"I don't think I do," said Carton. "I am a disappointed slave, sir. I care for no man on earth, and no man on earth cares for me."

"You might have used your talents better."

"Maybe so, Mr. Darnay, maybe not. Good night!"

Turning to his wine for comfort, Carton drank it all in a few minutes. Then he fell asleep with his head on his arms.

Just after ten o'clock at night, Carton tossed his hat on and walked out of the tavern. He paced the streets awhile to revive himself and then turned into Mr. Stryver's chambers.

Stryver opened the door wearing his slippers and a loose bed gown. They went into a dingy room lined with books and littered with papers.

"Get to work! Get to work!" Mr. Stryver

said. Stryver was a favorite at the Bar and Old Bailey. He was scheming, ready, and bold. But he had one flaw. He had not the ability to find the most important information from a heap of statements. This is one of the keys to being a lion among attorneys and Mr. Stryver was determined to be a lion.

Carton, the most unpromising of men, was Stryver's great assistant. Stryver never had a case without having Carton gather his points of

argument for him. It began to get around that, although Carton would never be a lion, he was an amazingly good jackal. It was time for the jackal to go to work.

"I am ready! How much to do?" Carton said.

"Only two sets of them," Mr. Stryver merrily said as he looked among his papers.

"Give me the worst first."

"There they are, Sydney. Fire away!" The lion then stretched himself out on the sofa. The jackal sat at the table, deeply focused on his task.

At last the jackal put together a legal summary for the lion and offered it to him. The lion took it and wrote his remarks on it with the jackal's help. Then the lion lay down to meditate and the jackal dug into the second stack of papers. The second case was not discussed and completed until the clocks struck three in the morning.

The jackal shook himself, yawned, and shivered. "And now, I'll get to bed."

CHAPTER
6

Monseigneur Marquis

"To the Devil with you!" the Marquis said, as he left the reception of one of the powerful lords in the French king's court. The Marquis was a handsomely dressed man of about sixty. He was haughty with a face like a fine pale mask. He got into his carriage and sped away.

His man drove as if he were charging an enemy. It seemed agreeable to the Marquis to see the common people fleeing from his horses. At last, swooping at a street corner by a fountain, one of the wheels gave a sickening little jolt.

There was a loud cry and the horses reared. The frightened valet got down in a hurry and there were twenty hands at the horses' bridles.

"What has gone wrong?" he asked calmly.

A tall man in a nightcap caught up a bundle from among the horses' feet. He lay it down on the fountain base and howled over it.

"Pardon, Monsieur the Marquis," said a ragged man, "it is his child."

The tall man came running at the carriage.

"Killed!" the man shrieked wildly at the Marquis.

The people closed around and looked at the Marquis. The Marquis ran his eyes over them all, as if they were mere rats coming out of their holes. He took out his purse.

"It is extraordinary to me that you people cannot take care of yourselves and your children. How do I know what injury you have done to my horses?"

He threw a gold coin for the valet to pick up. "Give him that."

The tall man called out again. "Dead!" Another man arrived and the miserable man leaned on his shoulder sobbing.

"I know all," said the latecomer. "Be a brave man, Gaspard! The poor thing has died in a moment and without pain. Could he have lived an hour as happily?"

"You are a philosopher, you there," said the Marquis smiling. "How do they call you?"

"Defarge."

The Marquis threw him another coin. "Pick that up, philosopher, and spend it as you will." He was just being driven away when a coin came flying into his carriage.

"You dogs!" said the Marquis. "I would ride over any one of you willingly." He leaned back in his seat again and gave the word to drive on.

The Marquis kept on his way into the countryside. It was a beautiful place, but it was a broken place. The Marquis looked about with the air of one who was coming home.

The village had its one poor street with its poor brewery, poor tannery, poor tavern, poor stable yard, and poor fountain. All the people were poor, too. Few children could be seen and no dogs. But there were plenty of taxes.

The Marquis drew up in his traveling carriage at the post house gate. The peasants stopped what they were doing to look at him. The Marquis cast his eyes over the faces when a grizzled man, a mender of the roads, joined the group.

"Bring me that fellow," said the Marquis to the messenger who traveled with him.

The fellow was brought, cap in hand.

"I passed you on the road. What did you look at so intently?"

"Monseigneur, I looked at the man." He stooped a little and pointed with his tattered blue cap under the carriage. "He swung by a chain under the carriage."

"Who?" demanded the traveler. "How do you call the man? You know all the men of this part of the country."

"Pardon! He was not of this part of the country."

"What was he like?"

"He was covered with dust and white as a ghost. A tall ghost! He threw himself over the hillside headfirst, as a man plunges into a river."

"Monsieur Gabelle, see to it!" Gabelle was

the postmaster and tax collector.

Gabelle bowed and said, "Monseigneur, I am flattered to devote myself to your service."

"Go on!" With a burst, the carriage started out of the village and up the hill. Soon the carriage stopped at the front door of a large house. The house was a stony place altogether. Stone urns, stone flowers, stone faces, and stone heads of lions decorated stone terraces, courtyards, and staircases. A torch was brought to light the Marquis's way in.

"Has Monsieur Charles arrived yet?"

"Monseigneur, not yet."

The great door clanged behind the Marquis. He crossed a hall filled with spears, swords, and knives on his way to his private apartment. The three rooms were luxurious with rich furniture and high vaulted ceilings. A supper table was set for two in a round room.

"I will dine in a quarter of an hour," the Marquis informed a servant.

Though his nephew had still not arrived, the Marquis sat down to his delicious supper. He was halfway through it, when his nephew came into the round room. He was known in England as Charles Darnay.

"You have been a long time coming," said the Marquis with a smile.

"I have been detained by business," the nephew explained.

"Without doubt," said the polished uncle.

"Sir, we have done wrong and are reaping the fruits of wrong."

"We have done wrong?" repeated the Marquis, delicately pointing to his nephew and then himself.

"Our family. Even in my father's time, we did a world of wrong. I am left bound to a system that is frightful to me."

"I will die supporting the system under which I have lived." The uncle's voice was quiet, but his face was cruel.

"This property and France are lost to me. I give them up," said the nephew sadly. "What is it but a wasteland of misery and ruin?"

"Hah!" said the Marquis, looking around the luxurious room. "How do you intend to live?"

"I must do what my countrymen, even with nobility, may have to do someday. Work."

"In England?"

"Yes. The family honor is safe from me in England. It is my refuge."

"You are tired," said the Marquis. "Good night! I look to the pleasure of seeing you again in the morning."

With that, the nephew was dismissed from the uncle's apartment. He commanded a servant, "Light the way for my nephew to his chamber." Then added quietly to himself, "And burn my nephew in his bed, if you will."

That night, the Marquis closed his thin bed curtains and went to sleep. In the village, the poor were fast asleep dreaming of banquets as the starved usually do.

The return of morning brought the return of everyday things, such as the carol of birds and the radiance of the sun. It also brought the unusual ringing of the great château bell, the trampling of feet on stairs and terrace, and the hasty saddling of horses and quick riding away.

In the stone house, another stony face had been added during the night. It lay on the pillow of Monsieur the Marquis. His face was like a fine mask, angry and hard. Driven into his heart was a knife. Scrawled on a frill of paper circling the hilt were the words: *Drive him fast to his tomb. From Jacques.*

Two Promises

A year had come and gone. Mr. Charles Darnay prospered in England as a tutor of the French language. He spent a good portion of his time in London and all of his time loving Lucie Manette.

He had loved Miss Manette from the hour of his trial but had not yet spoken of it to her. After spending some time in Cambridge, Darnay returned to London and went to speak to Doctor Manette. He knew Lucie to be out with Miss Pross.

Darnay found the doctor reading in his armchair by a window. The doctor was now an energetic man who studied much, slept little, and kept cheerful. As soon as Darnay entered, the doctor put aside his book.

"Charles Darnay! I rejoice to see you. Lucie has gone out, but she will soon be home."

"Doctor Manette, I knew she was away from home. I took the opportunity to speak to you."

"Is Lucie the topic?"

"Yes. Doctor Manette, I love your daughter. If ever there were love in the world, I love her!"

"I believe it," said Lucie's father. "I thought so before now."

"Do not believe, if one day I am so happy as to make her my wife, that I would put any separation between her and you. No, I look only to share your life and home and to be faithful to you to death."

"You speak so feelingly, Darnay, that I thank you with all my heart. If Lucie should ever tell me you are necessary for her happiness, I will give her to you."

"Your confidence in me begs me to tell you my own family name and why I am in England."

"Stop!" said the doctor. "Tell me when I ask you, not now. If Lucie loves you, you shall tell me on your marriage day. Do you promise?"

"Willingly."

"She will be home soon. Go! God bless you!"

<hr />

If Sydney Carton ever shone anywhere, he certainly never shone in the house of Doctor Manette. He had been there often during a whole year and was always the same moody visitor.

One day in August when Mr. Stryver had taken himself on vacation, Sydney came to the doctor's door. He found Lucie at her work, alone. She had never been quite at ease with him. But looking up at his face during greeting, she saw a change in it.

"I fear you are not well, Mr. Carton."

"No. But the life I lead, Miss Manette, is not a friend to health."

"Is it not a pity to live no better life? Why not change it?"

Looking gently at him, she was surprised to see tears in his eyes.

"It is too late for that. I shall never be better than I am." He leaned an elbow on her table and covered his eyes with his hand. "Will you hear me?"

"If it would make you happier, it would make me very glad."

"Bless you! If it was possible you could return the love of the man you see before you, he knows he would bring you to misery. I know very well you have no tenderness for me. I ask for none. I am even thankful it cannot be."

"I know you would say this to no one else," she said in tears. "Have I no power for your good at all?"

"The utmost good that I am capable of, Miss Manette, I have come here to offer. For you, and anyone dear to you, I would do anything. Outwardly, I will be as I have always been. But within myself I will always be, toward you, what I am right now. Believe this of me."

"I will, Mr. Carton."

He said, "Farewell! God bless you!" and left her.

CHAPTER 8

One Night

Mr. Cruncher usually sat on his stool watching people flow up and down Fleet Street. During the summer months, business slowed. One morning he noticed an unusual commotion pouring down the street.

"Young Jerry," said Cruncher to his son, "it's a buryin'. Get atop this here seat and look at the crowd."

His son obeyed. He saw the crowd approaching alongside a dingy hearse and a dingy mourners' coach. Only one mourner sat in the coach. The people swarmed around the coach, calling out, "Yah! Spies!"

Funerals always had a remarkable attraction for Cruncher. Finally, he learned the funeral was for one Roger Cly.

"Was he a spy?" asked Cruncher.

"Old Bailey spy," returned the man.

"Why to be sure!" exclaimed Cruncher, recalling the trial at which he had assisted Mr. Lorry. "I've seen him. He's dead, is he?"

"Dead as mutton!" said the man. And then he hollered, "Pull 'em out, there!"

The crowd mobbed the two vehicles until they had to stop. The one mourner scuffled out of his coach and barely avoided the crowd.

The tradesmen hurriedly shut up their shops. A crowd in those days stopped at nothing and was a monster to fear. Then someone suggested escorting the body to the church of Saint Pancras with rejoicing. The coach was immediately filled with eight people and one of them was Jerry Cruncher.

The disorderly procession brought the body of Roger Cly to its burying ground. After the crowd left the graveyard, Cruncher stayed behind to talk to the undertakers. On his way back to Tellson's, he paid a short visit to a well-known surgeon.

Young Jerry reported there had been no jobs while his father was gone. The bank closed and Cruncher and his son went home.

"Are you going out tonight?" asked Mrs. Cruncher, his decent wife.

"Yes, I am."

"May I go with you, Father?" asked his son.

"No, you mayn't. I'm a going fishing," Cruncher said, taking a bite of his bread and butter.

"Shall you bring any fish home, Father?

"That's questions enough for you," returned the father.

Much later young Jerry and then his mother were ordered to bed. At one o'clock in the morning, Cruncher rose from his chair, unlocked a cupboard, and took out a sack, a crowbar, a rope, a chain, and other fishing tackle of that nature. He put out the light and went out.

Young Jerry, who had only pretended to undress for bed, followed his father. Pulled along by the ambition to know the mystery of

his father's honest trade, young Jerry kept his
parent in view. His father was soon joined by
another man and the two trudged on. A half
hour from their home, another fisherman was
picked up.

The three men stopped and young Jerry crouched down to watch. He saw his parent climb an iron gate. The other two men went over and then all three moved away on their hands and knees. Young Jerry went up to the gate and crouched again, holding his breath.

The three fishermen were creeping through grass with gravestones looking on like ghosts. It was a large churchyard they were in. They stopped, stood upright, and began to fish.

They fished with a spade first. Cruncher then appeared to be adjusting an instrument like a great corkscrew. Whatever tools they worked with, they worked hard.

They seemed to have gotten a bite. Their bent bodies strained, as if by a heavy weight. Slowly the weight came to the surface.

Young Jerry knew well what it would be. But when he saw it, and saw his father about to wrench it open, he was so frightened he ran off. He didn't stop until he had run a mile or more. He went on as fast as his breath would allow until he scrambled into his bed.

There was no fish for breakfast and not much of anything else. Cruncher was in a temper, but he was brushed and washed at the usual hour. He set off with his son to pursue his work.

"Father, what's a Resurrection Man?" asked young Jerry, as they walked along.

Cruncher came to a stop. "How should I know?"

"I thought you knowed everything, Father," said the boy.

"Hem! Well, he's a tradesman," returned Cruncher.

"What's his goods?"

"His goods," said Cruncher after thinking, "is a branch of scientific goods."

"Persons' bodies, ain't it, Father?" asked the lively boy.

"I believe it is something of that sort."

"Oh, Father, I should so like to be a Resurrection Man someday when I'm quite growed up!"

Knitting

There was earlier activity than usual in the Saint Antoine wine shop of Monsieur Defarge. Madame Defarge sat in her seat with a bowl of battered small coins before her.

At noon two dusty men entered the shop. One was Monsieur Defarge. He greeted the men in the shop and said, "It is bad weather, gentlemen." The men all looked down and sat silent except one man, who got up and went out.

"My wife," said Defarge, "I have traveled miles with this good mender of roads called Jacques. I met him by accident a day and a half's journey out of Paris. Give him a drink!"

While the mender of roads drank his wine, two more men left the shop. Madame Defarge took up her knitting. The man finished his drink and a crust of dark bread.

Monsieur Defarge said, "Come! You shall see the apartment I told you about. It will suit you."

They went out of the shop and up a steep staircase to the high little room. The three men who had slipped out of the shop earlier were there.

Defarge closed the door and spoke quietly.

"This is the witness. He will tell you all. Speak, Jacques."

"I saw him a year ago underneath the carriage of the Marquis. Then the tall man was lost but they seek him. I finished work on the hillside, when I saw coming over the hill six soldiers. In the midst of them is a tall man with his arms tied to his side.

"When they came near to me, I recognized the tall man. I heard the chief say, 'Bring him fast to his tomb!' They started running faster toward the prison. In the morning I walked by the prison on the way to my work. There I saw him, high up, in a lofty cage."

Defarge and the three men looked at each other darkly.

"He remained in his cage for some days. On Sunday night while the village is asleep, soldiers came down from the prison. Workmen dug, workmen hammered, and the soldiers laughed. In the morning by the fountain there was a gallows forty feet high.

"At midday we heard the roll of the drums. He was hanged there and left hanging. It was frightful, messieurs. How can the women and children draw water? I left at sunset and walked until I met the comrade."

After a gloomy silence one of the Jacques said, "You have acted and spoken faithfully. Will you wait for us outside the door?"

"Willingly," said the mender of roads. He sat at the top of the stairs while the others talked.

"How say you, Jacques?" demanded one. "To be registered?"

"Yes, doomed to destruction," returned Defarge.

"The château and all the family?"

"Yes, completely wiped out," said Defarge.

Jacques Two asked, "Are you sure we shall always be able to decode the register? Or I ought to say, will she?"

Defarge answered, "Knitted in her own stitches and symbols, the register will always be as plain as day to my wife."

Soon after this the Defarges picked their way through the black mud streets in Saint Antoine. Madame asked her husband, "Say then, what did Jacques of the police tell thee?"

"Very little tonight, but there is another spy assigned to our area."

"Eh, well!" said Madame Defarge. "It is necessary to register him. What is he called?"

"He is English. His name is John Barsad."

"Good. Is his appearance known?"

"Age is about forty years. Height is about five feet nine. Black hair and eyes dark. Rather handsome but having a nose with a strange tilt towards the left cheek."

"It is a portrait!" said madame, laughing. "He shall be registered tomorrow."

Noon the next day saw the woman in her usual place in the wine shop, knitting away. A rose lay beside her. A figure entering at the door threw a shadow on Madame Defarge. She laid down her knitting and pinned her rose in her headdress before she looked up.

It was curious. The moment she took up the rose, the customers ceased talking and began to slowly drop out of the shop.

"Good day, madame," said the newcomer.

"Good day, monsieur," she said aloud. Thinking, *Hah! Good day age about forty, five feet nine, black hair and dark eyes with nose leaning toward the left cheek!*

The man asked for a drink and lingered to watch the woman knit. "You knit with great skill, madame. A pretty pattern, too."

"You think so?" said madame, looking at him with a smile.

John, thought madame, checking off her work as her fingers knitted. Stay long enough and I shall knit *Barsad* before you go.

The man did stay long enough, sipping his drink and asking questions. After Monsieur Defarge entered the shop, he turned his questions to the shop owner. He eventually said, "I have the honor of cherishing some interesting associations with your name."

"Indeed!" said Defarge, with no emotion.

"Yes, I have known Doctor Manette and his daughter in England."

"Yes?" said Defarge.

"She is to marry the nephew of Monsieur the Marquis, for whom Gaspard was hung so high," offered the spy. "In other words, the present Marquis. In England he is known as Charles Darnay."

Madame Defarge knitted steadily, but the news had a clear effect on her husband. Having made his one hit, the spy paid for his drink and departed.

"Can it be true?" said Defarge in a low voice.

"It is probably false, but it may be true," returned the madame.

"Is it not strange, that for all our sympathy for her father and herself, her husband's name should be condemned under your hand at this moment by the side of that spy dog who has just left us?"

Echoing Footsteps

The wedding day shone brightly. The beautiful bride, Mr. Lorry, and Miss Pross were ready to go to the church. They waited outside the closed door of the doctor's room, where he was speaking with Charles Darnay.

The door opened and the men came out. The doctor was deadly pale, but he gave his arm to his daughter to escort her to the waiting chariot. The small group rode to a nearby church, where Lucie Manette and Charles Darnay were happily married.

When the newly married pair came home from their wedding trip, Sydney Carton was the first to give his congratulations. He watched for an opportunity to speak to Darnay alone.

"Mr. Darnay," said Carton, "I wish for us to be friends."

"We are already friends, I hope."

"You are good to say so. If you can endure to have such a worthless fellow coming and going, I ask for the privilege to do so. I doubt I would come but four or so times in a year."

"Will you try?"

"That is another way of granting what I have asked. I thank you, Darnay." They shook hands on it.

When Mr. Carton had gone, Lucie remarked to her husband, "There is scarcely a hope Mr. Carton's ways can be repaired now. But I am still sure he is capable of good things."

⚜⚜⚜

A wonderful corner for echoes was that corner where the doctor and his family lived. Lucie heard in the echoes only friendly sounds. Her husband's footsteps were strong and prosperous. Her father's were firm and equal. Soon came the tread of tiny feet from a daughter, little Lucie, as she chattered in the languages of the two cities blended in her life.

But other echoes began rumbling like a menace. It was near the time of little Lucie's sixth birthday that the awful sound of a dreadful storm in France grew.

On a night in mid-July 1789, Mr. Lorry came in late from Tellson's Bank and sat with Lucie and Charles.

"I began to think I would have to work through the night at Tellson's," Lorry said. "There is such uneasiness in Paris that we've had quite a run in business. Our customers there cannot send their property to us in England fast enough."

"That has a bad look to it," said Darnay.

"Yes, but we don't know the reason for it. Now let us sit quiet and listen to the echoes."

Footsteps raged in Saint Antoine, far from the little circle sitting in London. A forest of arms clutched at weapons being given out. Voices echoed around Defarge's wine shop, where Monsieur Defarge issued orders.

"Where is my wife?" he cried.

"Here you see me!" said Madame. Her right hand held an ax and in her belt were a pistol and a knife. "You shall see me at the head of the women, by and by."

"Come then, patriots and friends!" shouted Defarge. "To the Bastille!"

A sea of people rose and overflowed the city. Alarm bells rang, drums beat, and the attack began.

"To me, women!" cried Madame Defarge. "We can kill as well as the men when the place is taken!"

Cannon, muskets, fire, and smoke raged for hours. A white flag and lowered drawbridge found Defarge swept into the eight surrendered towers.

"The prisoners! The records! The secret cells!" These cries were taken up by those who rushed in, taking the prison officers with them. Defarge separated one of these officers from the rest and pressed him against a wall.

"Show me the North Tower! One Hundred and Five North Tower, quick!"

"This way," the man said. He led Defarge through gloomy passages, up and down steps. The man put a key into the lock and swung a low door open.

"Pass that torch slowly along those walls that I might see them," Defarge ordered the officer.

"Stop! Look here. A. M. Alexandre Manette," said Defarge. After searching the cell, they rejoined the raging flood of people. When Defarge returned to the head of the mob, they marched on to take the governor of the Bastille to the Hotel de Ville for judgment.

At the end of the day there were two groups of seven faces. Seven faces of prisoners, released by the storm that had burst open their cages. Seven dead faces were carried higher, on the tops of pikes. These were escorted with loudly echoing footsteps through the Paris streets.

Monsieur Defarge said to his wife in a husky tone, "At last it is come, my dear!"

CHAPTER
11

In Secret

Three more birthdays were celebrated in young Lucie's peaceful life. Three more years of reports about the terror in their birthplace worried her parents and grandfather. It was August 1792. Royalty was gone and the nobility had been scattered far and wide.

A good many of the monseigneurs gathered at Tellson's Bank in London. The bank had become the most reliable source for the latest French news. On a steaming afternoon, Mr. Lorry sat at his desk and Charles Darnay leaned on it, speaking with him in a low voice.

"Unsettled weather, a long journey, uncertain means of traveling, a country and city that may not be safe for you," Darnay listed his reasons for Mr. Lorry not to travel to Paris.

"My dear Charles, you have no idea the difficulty if our bank documents are taken or destroyed by fire! It is safe enough for me. No one will interfere with an old fellow."

"How I admire your youthful spirit, Mr. Lorry. Will you take no one with you?"

"I intend to take Jerry. He has been my bodyguard for a long time."

As Mr. Lorry paused, another employee approached him and laid a soiled, unopened letter before him. The man asked Mr. Lorry if he had been able to discover any clues of the man to which it was addressed. The letter was so close to Charles he could read: "Very urgent. To Monsieur the Marquis St. Evremonde, of France."

Mr. Lorry responded, "No one can tell me where this gentleman is to be found."

"I know the fellow," said Darnay.

"Will you take the letter?" asked Mr. Lorry.

"I will. Do you start for Paris from here?"

"Yes, from here at eight."

"I will come back to see you off." Darnay then made his way to a quiet place, opened the letter and read.

It was written by Monsieur Gabelle from the prison of the Abbaye in Paris. He wrote:

Monsieur the Marquis,

I have been seized with great violence and brought to Paris. The crime for which I am imprisoned is, they tell me, treason against the people by my service for you. It is in vain that I insist I acted for them, not against.

For the love of Heaven, for justice, and for the honor of your noble name, I beg you to come help me.

Your miserable servant,
GABELLE

Monsieur Gabelle had served the estate as Darnay had instructed to spare the villagers as much hardship as possible. The appeal of the innocent prisoner drew him. He was decided. He must go to Paris.

That night he sat up late and wrote two tender letters. One was to Lucie explaining why he had to go to Paris. The other was to the doctor placing Lucie and their dear child in his care.

The next day passed quickly. Early in the evening, Darnay embraced his wife and child, telling them he would return by and by. He left

the letters with a trusted messenger to be delivered before midnight. Picking up a valise of clothes he had hidden earlier, he took a horse for Dover. His journey had begun.

The traveler fared slowly. The changed times brought much more delay than rough roads and bad horses. Every town and village had its own band of patriots who stopped all who came and went.

Darnay had journeyed for days when he stopped at a small town for a night of sleep. The men at the guardhouse gave him such difficulty that he was not surprised to be woken up in the middle of the night by a local representative. Three armed men in red caps were with him.

"Emigrant, I am going to send you on to Paris with an escort," said the representative. "You are an aristocrat and must pay for it."

Darnay was taken back to the guardhouse to pay a heavy price for the escort. He and his two patriot escorts, who carried sabers and muskets, started on the road. The rest of the journey to

Paris they traveled at night through sharp rain and sometimes sharp crowds who cried out, "Down with the emigrant!"

At last, one day at sunrise they came to the wall of Paris.

"Where are the papers of this prisoner?" demanded a man in authority.

One of the patriots produced them. The man glanced at them, showed some surprise, and looked closely at Darnay. He left the three waiting on their horses and went into the guardroom.

The man came back and ordered Darnay to dismount his horse. Darnay did so and the two escorts turned and led his horse away without entering the city.

Darnay was taken into the guardroom. There, he faced a desk managed by a dark, coarse officer.

"Citizen Defarge," the officer said to Darnay's new escort, "is this the emigrant Evremonde?"

"This is the man."

"Evremonde, you are assigned to the prison of La Force."

"Under what law and for what offense?" asked Darnay.

The officer looked up from his writing. "We have new laws and offenses since you were here last," he said with a hard smile.

The officer finished writing and handed the slip of paper to Defarge that said, "In secret."

As they went down the guardroom steps Defarge said in a low voice, "Is it you who married the daughter of Doctor Manette?"

"Yes," replied Darnay, surprised.

"My name is Defarge. Possibly you have heard of me."

"My wife came to you to be reunited with her father? Yes!"

"In the name of that new sharp female called La Guillotine, why did you come to France?"

"I am not to be buried there, without any means of presenting my case?"

"You will see. But, why not? Other people have been buried in worse prisons before now."

"Never by me, Citizen Defarge."

They walked on in a steady silence. With the separation from his wife and child on his mind, Darnay arrived at the prison of La Force. A man opened the strong gate.

Defarge presented his prisoner, "The emigrant Evremonde."

The man exclaimed, "What the Devil! How many more of them?"

Looking at the written paper he grumbled, "In secret too! As if I was not already full to bursting!" He took up his keys and led Darnay to a low black door. They passed into a single cell that was cold and damp but not dark.

"Yours," said the jailer.

"Why am I confined alone?"

"How should I know?" he answered and left.

Now I am left, as if dead, Darnay thought as he walked in his cell.

CHAPTER
12

Calm in the Storm

Tellson's Bank in Paris was in a wing of a large house. The house had belonged to a great nobleman who dressed himself in his cook's dress to get across the borders. The patriots were now in possession of the building and used the other wings for their horrid business.

Mr. Lorry occupied rooms in the bank and did his duty for his employers. On the opposite side of the courtyard stood a large grindstone. Mr. Lorry looked at it through his window and then closed the shutters, shivering. The bell at the gate sounded. He was surprised when Lucie and her father rushed through the door.

Lucie gasped, "My dear friend! An errand of kindness brought my husband here unknown to us. He was sent to prison!"

Their old friend uttered a cry. Almost at the same moment the bell rang again and the noise of feet and voices poured into the courtyard.

"What is that noise?" asked the doctor, turning toward the window.

"Don't look out!" cried Mr. Lorry.

The doctor gave him a bold smile. "My friend, I have a charmed life in Paris. My imprisonment in the Bastille has given me power among the patriots. I know I can help Charles."

"Lucie," said Mr. Lorry, "let me put you in a room at the back here. You must not delay."

Lucie let her old friend rush her into his room. He hurried back to the doctor and partially opened the shutter to give him a view into the courtyard.

A throng of forty or fifty men and women poured in to work at the grindstone. With cruel faces they sharpened their weapons. Hatchets, knives, bayonets, and swords were brought to be sharpened and they were all stained red. When deadly sharp again, the weapons were snatched up and their owners sprinted away into the streets.

"They are murdering prisoners," whispered Mr. Lorry. "If you really have the power to help Charles, make yourself known to these devils and get taken to La Force prison. Now!"

Doctor Manette hurried out. There was a pause among the crowd as he captured their attention. Then he was escorted out with cries of "Long live the Bastille prisoner! Help for the Bastille prisoner's kin at La Force!"

Mr. Lorry went quickly to Lucie and told her that her father had gone in search of her husband with the people's help.

The next day, Mr. Lorry found lodging for his friends high up in a building on a calmer street. After giving them what comfort he could, he left Jerry Cruncher to watch the doorway. Then, he returned to the bank.

After the bank closed and Mr. Lorry was alone in his rooms, he heard a foot on the stair. In a moment a man with dark, curling hair stood before him and addressed him by name.

"You have come from Doctor Manette?" Mr. Lorry asked.

"Yes." Defarge put into his hand a scrap of paper. In the doctor's writing it read: *Charles is safe but I cannot safely leave this place yet.*

Doctor Manette did not return for four days. During that time 1,100 prisoners were killed by the people. When he arrived at La Force prison, he found a group of men and women who had appointed themselves as the court. Prisoners were brought one by one before the court and the court decided if they were to be killed, released, or sent back to their cell.

The doctor had introduced himself to the court and was identified by one of its members, Defarge. He asked for the release of Charles Darnay but was told Darnay must remain in prison for now. It was promised he would remain safely.

Doctor Manette stayed at the prison and used his skills as a physician wisely. He was soon the inspecting physician of three prisons, including La Force.

The doctor saw Lucie's husband weekly and brought home messages to her. He was able to tell her Charles was now allowed to mix with the other prisoners. Although the doctor tried hard to get him set free, the public feeling against him was too strong.

A new period had begun. The king was tried, doomed, and beheaded by La Guillotine. After eight months in prison, his wife was also.

The hideous figure of the sharp La Guillotine grew familiar, as if it had existed from the beginning of the world. It struck down the once powerful, the beautiful, and the good. Among these terrors walked Doctor Manette with a steady head. No man was better known in Paris than the doctor at that time or more respected. He never doubted he would save Charles.

Triumph

One year and three months passed. Lucie was never sure that La Guillotine might not strike off her husband's head the next day. Every day, carts rumbled through the stony streets filled with the condemned. Not giving into despair, Lucie remained true to her duties.

They had not been in their new lodgings many weeks when her father told her, "My dear, there is an upper window in the prison. Charles can sometimes get to it at three in the afternoon. If you stand in a certain place in the street, he thinks he might be able to see you. You will not see him, sadly, and it would not be safe for you to make any sign."

"Oh, show me the place, Father. I will go there every day."

From that time on, she waited there two hours in all kinds of weather. She never missed a single day. When the weather was nice, she brought little Lucie. Her father said Charles did see her when he was able to get to the window.

On a lightly snowing day in December she arrived at the usual corner. Her father met her there.

"I left Charles climbing to the window. Since there is no one here in the street, you may kiss your hand toward the highest roof."

"I do so, Father, and send my soul with it!"

A footstep crunched in the snow behind them just as Lucie made her sign.

"I salute you, Citizeness," said the doctor.

"I salute you, Citizen," Madame said in passing. Then she was gone like a shadow over the white road.

"Give me your arm, my love," said the doctor. "Charles is summoned before the court tomorrow. I have promising information. You are not afraid?"

She could barely answer, "I trust in you."

"Do so. He shall be restored to you."

There was a heavy sound of wheels not far off. They both knew too well what it meant. Three carts were taking away their doomed loads over the snow.

The next day, fifteen prisoners went before the court ahead of Charles. All fifteen were condemned and the trials for all of them took only one and a half hours.

"Charles Evremonde, called Darnay," was at length called.

Darnay's judges sat on the bench in feathered hats. Doctor Manette and Mr. Lorry sat below the president of the court.

Charles Evremonde was accused by the public attorney of being an emigrant, having left France to live in England.

"Take off his head!" yelled the audience. "An enemy to the Republic!"

The president rang his bell for quiet and asked the prisoner whether it was true that he had lived many years in England and why.

Darnay explained he had given up the noble title because it was distasteful to him. He left France to earn his living by his own effort in England, rather than being a burden to the people of France.

What proof did he have?

He gave the names of two witnesses, Theophile Gabelle and Alexandre Manette.

But he had married in England?

True, but not an Englishwoman.

A citizeness of France?

Yes, by birth.

Her name and family?

"Lucie Manette, only daughter of Doctor Manette, the good physician who sits there."

This answer had an amazing effect on the audience. Cheers were raised for the good doctor and people were moved to tears.

The president asked, "Why did you return to France when you did, and not earlier?"

Darnay replied he had not returned sooner simply because he had no way of earning a living in France. He had returned when he did to save a citizen's life and speak the truth on his behalf. Was that criminal in the Republic's eye?

The audience cried heartily, "NO!"

Monsieur Gabelle then testified that he had been the citizen in need. His letter to Darnay was found among the papers before the president.

The doctor was questioned next. His clear answers showed how the accused had remained

with him and his daughter during his exile from France after his long imprisonment. The court told the president it had heard enough and was ready to vote.

All the voices were in the prisoner's favor and the president declared him free!

When Darnay came out of the prison, a crowd rushed at him in celebration. They put him into a large chair decorated with a red flag and carried him all the way to the courtyard of their lodging.

After Darnay grasped the doctor's hand, grasped the hand of Mr. Lorry, kissed little Lucie, and embraced the faithful Miss Pross, he took his wife in his arms.

"Lucie! My own! I am safe," he said. "No other man in all of France could have done what your father did for me."

She laid her head on her father's chest. He said to her, "Don't tremble so. I have saved him."

A Knock at the Door

Miss Pross was waiting for Jerry Cruncher as he entered the family's apartment. She and Cruncher had the task of doing the daily shopping.

"Pray, be cautious!" cried Lucie.

They went out with Miss Pross carrying the money and Cruncher the basket. Lucie, her husband, her father, and her child sat by a bright fire.

"What is that?!" Lucie interrupted.

"My dear, settle down," said her father, laying his hand on hers.

"I thought I heard strange feet on the stairs."

Just then, a blow struck the door. Four armed men in red caps entered the room.

"Citizen Evremonde, called Darnay," said the

first. "You are again the prisoner of the Republic. You will return to the prison."

Doctor Manette grabbed the front of the man's shirt and said, "Will you tell me who accused him?"

"He is accused by the Citizen and Citizeness Defarge. And by one other."

"What other?"

"You will be answered tomorrow," said the man with a strange look.

As Darnay was being taken away, Miss Pross and Cruncher threaded their way along the narrow streets. They purchased a few items. Miss Pross then stopped at a shop called the Good Republican Brutus of Antiquity. It had a quieter look than any other they had seen.

They approached the counter and showed what they wanted. As they waited, a man rose to leave. No sooner did he face Miss Pross, than she screamed. In a moment everyone in the shop was on their feet.

"What is the matter?" asked the man in English, speaking in a low, vexed voice.

"Oh, Solomon!" cried Miss Pross. "After not hearing of you for so long, do I find you here?"

"Don't call me Solomon. Do you want to be the death of me?" asked the man. "Hold your tongue, and come outside."

As Miss Pross paid, Solomon offered a few words of explanation in French to the people in the shop. The three stepped outside.

"If you really don't want to risk my life, go your way and let me go mine. I am busy."

Miss Pross cried, "Say but one affectionate word to me and I'll not keep you."

He was saying the affectionate word far too grudgingly when Cruncher touched his shoulder.

"I say! May I ask whether your name is John Solomon or Solomon John?"

Solomon turned toward him with sudden distrust.

"Speak out," said Cruncher. "Your sister calls you Solomon. I know you're John. And about that name of Pross. That warn't your name over the water."

"What do you mean?"

"You was a spy witness at the Bailey. What was you called?"

"Barsad," said another voice.

"That's the name!" yelled Cruncher. The new speaker was Sydney Carton.

"Don't be alarmed, Miss Pross. I arrived at Mr. Lorry's to his surprise. I wish for your sake Mr. Barsad was not a sheep of the prisons."

Sheep was a common word for a spy. The sheep turned pale.

"Mr. Barsad!" exclaimed Carton. "I have a proposal I wish to make to you alone. Will you go with me to Tellson's Bank?"

"Yes, I'll hear what you have to say."

"I propose we bring your sister safely to the corner of her own street first. Come then!"

Mr. Lorry had finished his dinner and was sitting in front of a cheery fire. Carton told him the news of Darnay's arrest and introduced Miss Pross's brother. Mr. Lorry remembered his face from the trial in England.

Carton told the spy, "This is a desperate time,

when desperate games are played for desperate prizes. The prize I am determined to play for is a friend in the prison."

"You need to have good cards, sir," said the spy.

"I'll see what cards I hold," Carton said. "Sheep of the prisons are now employed by the Republican French army, but Mr. Barsad is suspected to still be in the pay of the English government as a spy. Are you following?"

"Not entirely," returned the spy, somewhat uneasily. Barsad saw losing cards Carton knew nothing about. Most damaging was his time as spy for the overthrown government. He remembered Madame Defarge with fear and had seen her condemn people to death with her knitted register.

"I think I have another good card here. That friend and fellow sheep you were speaking with earlier, who was he?"

"French. You don't know him," said the spy quickly.

"Yet I know the face." Carton struck his

open hand on the table. "Cly! We had him before us at the Old Bailey."

"Cly has been dead several years," said Barsad with a smile. "He was buried at the church of Saint Pancras. I happen to have with me the certificate of his burial. I helped lay him in the coffin."

Cruncher rose and stood at the spy's side. "That there Roger Cly," he said. "You put him in his coffin?"

"I did."

"Who took him out of it?"

Barsad leaned back in his chair and stammered, "What do you mean?"

"You buried stones and dirt in that there coffin," said Cruncher. "Cly warn't never in it. Me and two others know it."

"I give up," returned the spy. "We were so unpopular it was the only way Cly could get away. Though how this man knows it was a fake is a wonder. Now, what do you want with me?"

"You are a turnkey at the prison?"

"Sometimes."

Carton said, "So far we have spoken before these two men. It was good that the value of the cards should not rest only between you and me. Come into the dark room here and let us have a final word alone."

While Carton and the sheep of the prisons were in the next room, Mr. Lorry turned to Cruncher. He angrily shook a forefinger at him.

"I suspect you have had an unlawful business of a shameful kind. If you have, don't expect me to accept you when you get back to England. Tellson's shall not be burdened."

"What I humbly offer to you, sir, would be this: on that stool let my boy sit when he's growed up. Let his father go into the line of regular digging and make up for what he might have un-dug. I beg you to bear in mind that what I said earlier, I might have kept back."

"That at least is true," said Mr. Lorry. "Say no more now. Perhaps I shall yet stay your friend, if you deserve it and repent in action."

Carton and the spy returned. "Farewell, Mr. Barsad, you have nothing to fear from me."

When they were alone, Mr. Lorry asked Carton what he had done.

"Not much. If it goes ill with the prisoner, I have secured entry to him for one time."

Mr. Lorry's face fell. "If it should go ill, that will not save him."

"I never said it would. Your bank duties here have come to an end, sir?" said Carton.

"Yes. I have done all I can. I have my official Leave to Pass. Are you going out tonight?"

"You know my restless habits. I shall reappear in the morning. You go to the court tomorrow?"

"Yes, unhappily."

Carton left Mr. Lorry and walked. He stopped at a druggist's shop. It was a small, dim, crooked shop kept by a small, dim, crooked man. Certain small packages were made and given to him. He put them one by one inside his coat and counted out the money for them.

"There is nothing more for me to do until tomorrow," he said, glancing up at the moon. "I can't sleep."

He walked all night.

CHAPTER
15

Dusk

The court was all stirred up when the sheep pressed into a crowded corner. Mr. Lorry and Doctor Manette were there. She was there, sitting beside her father. When her husband was brought in, she turned a loving and tender look on him for encouragement.

The jury contained the same determined patriots as the day before and every day.

The president asked, "Is the prisoner openly accused or secretly?"

Mr. Public Prosecutor answered, "Openly, President."

"By whom?"

"Three voices. Ernest Defarge, wine merchant of Saint Antoine, Therese Defarge, his wife, and Alexandre Manette, doctor."

A great uproar took place in the court. Doctor Manette stood.

"President, I protest! Who and where is the false person who says I accuse the husband of my child!"

The president rang his bell. "Listen to what is to follow and be silent!"

Defarge was called for questioning.

"You did good service at the taking of the Bastille, citizen?"

"I believe so."

"Inform the jury what you did that day in the Bastille."

"I knew this former prisoner had been kept in a cell known as One Hundred and Five, North Tower. I decided to examine that cell. In a hole in the chimney I found a written paper. This is that paper. It is in the handwriting of Doctor Manette."

"Let it be read."

Doctor Manette's account of the events leading to his long imprisonment was read. He wrote of a night in December 1757, when two men from the noble Evremonde family pressured him into traveling to a country house. There, he found a young woman and a young man who were both dying. The young man told the doctor of the horrible deeds of the two noblemen, one a Marquis and the other his brother.

He told of his beautiful sister who had been recently married but had also caught the eye of the younger nobleman. The nobleman hitched the husband to a cart and worked him until he died. The sister was then taken away from her mourning family. Her father's heart burst under the loss.

Enraged, the youth first took his younger sister and hid her where she could not be found. Then he took an old soldier's sword to confront the nobleman. To the disgust of the nobleman he was forced to defend himself and gave the youth a deadly wound in the chest.

Before he breathed his last, the boy spoke to the Marquis as the doctor held him up, "In the days when all these things are to be answered for, I summon you and yours, to the last of your bad race, to answer for them."

The sister lingered in a fever for a week but also died. The Marquis offered the doctor gold, but he would not take it. When the doctor attempted to alert authorities about the dark events, the nobles had him secretly taken and imprisoned in the Bastille.

The account ended with the words, "Them and their descendants, I, Alexandre Manette, do denounce to the times when all things shall be answered for."

A terrible sound rose when the reading of the document was done.

"Much influence around him has the doctor," murmured Madame Defarge. "Save him now, my doctor!"

At every juryman's vote, there was a roar. Charles Darnay was by family an aristocrat and an enemy of the Republic. Death within twenty-four hours!

CHAPTER 16

Darkness

The judges and crowd poured out to the street. Lucie stretched her arms toward Charles. Barsad proposed to the few officials left, "Let her embrace him for a moment."

Charles folded her into his arms. "Farewell, darling of my soul. We shall meet again, where the weary are at rest!"

"I can bear it, dear Charles. I am supported from above. Don't suffer for me."

Her father began to fall on his knees before them. Darnay grabbed him, crying, "No! What have you done, that you should kneel to us? We know now what you went through when you learned my family name. We know the natural hatred you conquered for her sake. We thank you with all our hearts!"

The doctor's only answer was a shriek of anguish. As Darnay was drawn away, his wife stood looking after him with a comforting smile. He went out at the prisoners' door. She turned to her father and fell at his feet.

Carton came out of his corner to pick her up. "Shall I take her to a coach?" he asked her father and Mr. Lorry.

When they arrived at their building, Carton carried her to their rooms. He laid her down on the couch, where her child and Miss Pross wept over her.

He arranged to meet Mr. Lorry at Tellson's at nine o'clock that evening. Mr. Lorry followed Carton to the outside door.

"I have no hope," said Mr. Lorry in a low and sorrowful whisper.

"Nor have I," said Carton, as he stepped through the doorway. Carton paused in the street, deciding what to do until nine o'clock.

"Shall I show myself to these people? It may be a necessary step. But care, care!" He turned his steps toward the Saint Antoine section. He found a place to eat dinner and fell sound asleep until seven o'clock.

Rested, he went to Defarge's wine shop. The only other customers were one of the men on the jury and a woman. They were talking with both of the Defarges.

Carton took his seat and asked in poor French for some wine. Madame Defarge cast a careless glance at him and then a closer one. She went to him and asked what he had ordered. He repeated what he had already said.

Madame Defarge returned to her counter to get the wine. He heard her say, "I swear to you, like Evremonde!"

Monsieur Defarge brought him the wine and gave him a "Good Evening."

"Oh! Good evening, Citizen. I drink to the Republic." Carton filled his glass and then took out a newspaper. Following a line of print with a finger, he showed a face of concentration. The group at the counter resumed their talk.

"Well," reasoned Defarge, "one must stop somewhere. The question is still where?"

"At extinction," said madame.

"In general, I say nothing against it," said Defarge, rather troubled. "But this doctor has suffered much. You saw his face when the paper was read."

"I have seen his face to not be the face of a true friend of the Republic," said madame, angrily. "Let him take care of his face!"

"And you saw the agony of his daughter, which must be an agony to him!"

"Yes, I have seen his daughter. I have seen her in court and I have seen her in the street by the prison. You would rescue the man even now," she told her husband.

"No!" he protested. "I would stop there."

Madame Defarge said to the other two at the counter, "In the beginning of the great days when the Bastille fell, I told my husband a secret. I told him that peasant family so injured by the two Evremonde brothers is my family. Those dead are my dead. So tell Wind and Fire where to stop but don't tell me."

Other customers came in, ending the talk.

The English customer paid for his wine and went on his way, first to the prison and then to Mr. Lorry's rooms. Carton told him Lucie and her daughter were in danger from Madame Defarge.

"Don't look so horrified. You will save them all," Carton said.

"Heaven grant I may, Carton! But how?"

"Early tomorrow have your horses ready to travel at two o'clock. Press upon Lucie the necessity of taking her child and father out of Paris for their safety."

"It shall be done!"

"You are a noble heart. Have the carriage in the courtyard here and wait in your seat. Here, take my traveling papers with the others. Wait for nothing but to have my place occupied, and then for England!'"

"I hope to do my part faithfully."

"And I hope to do mine. Now, good-bye!" Carton said with a grave smile.

As he crossed the courtyard, he breathed a blessing and a farewell toward Lucie's room.

CHAPTER 17

The Knitting Done

When Charles Darnay awoke, it flashed in his mind, *This is the day of my death!* Fifty-two heads were to fall at three o'clock. Darnay walked to and fro as the clocks struck numbers he would never hear again.

One o'clock had just struck away when he heard footsteps. The door was quickly opened and closed and before him stood Sydney Carton with a warning finger on his lip.

"I bring a request from your wife. You must obey." Carton told Darnay to exchange his boots, coat, and scarf with his own.

Darnay did as he asked, protesting, "Dear Carton, this is madness!"

"Quick, sit down and write what I tell you."

Bewildered, Darnay sat at his desk and

wrote. Carton's hand dipped close to Darnay's face several times as he formed the words. Then the pen dropped from Darnay's hand.

"What vapor is that?" he asked.

"I am aware of nothing."

Within a minute Darnay was stretched insensible on the ground. Carton softly called, "Come in!" The spy presented himself. "Take him to the courtyard and place him in the carriage. Tell Mr. Lorry he only needs air to be restored."

The spy brought two men and they carried Darnay out. Barsad closed the door and Carton was left alone until the jailer opened his cell, saying, "Follow me, Evremonde."

As the fifty-two waited in a large dark room, a young woman with a sweet spare face came to speak to Carton. "Citizen Evremonde, I am a poor seamstress who was with you in La Force. Will you let me hold your hand? I am little and weak; it will give me courage."

As her patient eyes were lifted to his face, he saw sudden doubt and then amazement.

"Are you dying for him?" she whispered.

"And his wife and child. Hush! Yes."

"Oh, will you let me hold your brave hand, stranger?"

"Hush! Yes, my poor sister; to the last."

At that same hour a coach going out of Paris drove up to the barrier to be examined. Jarvis Lorry handed out their papers to be read and answered the official's questions.

"You can depart. A good journey!"

"I salute you, citizen," said Mr. Lorry.

"Are we not going too slowly?" asked Lucie, clinging to her old friend.

"I must not urge them too much. It would spark suspicion."

The wind rushed after them. The clouds flew after them. But they were pursued by nothing else.

Madame Defarge took herself along the streets toward the doctor's lodging. Under her robe she had hidden a pistol at her chest and a dagger at her waist. She planned to catch Lucie grieving for her husband.

Only Miss Pross and Jerry Cruncher remained at the lodging, preparing to leave the city in a fast carriage. Miss Pross worried about awaking suspicion by having two vehicles leaving from the courtyard so close together.

"Cruncher, go stop the horses and carriage from coming here. Take me in by the cathedral door instead."

"I am doubtful about leaving you," said Cruncher.

"Have no fear for me. Be at the cathedral at three o'clock. Bless you, Cruncher!"

Cruncher went out and Miss Pross set about getting ready to leave. She paused to look about the room and cried out, for she saw a figure standing in the shadows.

Madame Defarge looked coldly at her, and said in French, "Where is the wife of Evremonde?"

"You shall not get the better of me. I am an Englishwoman," Miss Pross answered in English.

There were four doors leading out the room. While the French woman checked three empty rooms, the English woman planted herself before the last.

"I will tear you to pieces, but I will have you from that door," said Madame Defarge. She lunged at the door.

Miss Pross clasped her tight around the waist and lifted her off the floor in the struggle. Madame Defarge's hands went to her chest. Miss Pross saw what was there and struck at it. After a flash and a crash, she stood alone.

As the smoke cleared, it passed out on the air like the soul of the furious woman whose body lay lifeless. Miss Pross grabbed her things, locked the front door, and hurried away. While crossing a bridge, she dropped the key in the river. At the cathedral, the carriage appeared and took her in.

"Is there any noise in the streets?" she asked Mr. Cruncher.

"Hark! There's the roll of them dreadful carts! You can hear that, miss?"

"I can hear nothing," said Miss Pross, seeing he had spoken to her. She never did hear anything else in this world.

In front of La Guillotine sat many women in chairs, busily knitting and counting each head taken. One chair remained empty as the supposed Evremonde and the seamstress stood in the fast-shrinking crowd of victims. He still held her hand as he had promised.

"Keep your eyes on me, dear child, and mind nothing else," said Carton.

"You comfort me so much! Is the moment come?"

"Yes."

She went before him. The knitting women counted twenty-two.

The murmuring of many voices, the upturning of many faces, all flashed away. Twenty-three.

They said of him, that his was the most peaceful man's face ever seen there.

"It is a far, far better thing I do, than I have ever done. It is a far, far better rest I go to than I have ever known."